This book belongs to

....

For Y.

RED FOX

UK I USA I Canada I Ireland I Australia I India I New Zealand I South Africa

Red Fox is part of the Penguin Random House group of companies
whose addresses can be found at global.penguinrandomhouse.com.

www.penguin.co.uk   www.puffin.co.uk   www.ladybird.co.uk

 Penguin
Random House
UK

First published 2009
This edition published 2018
001

Printed in China
A CIP catalogue record for this book is available from the British Library

ISBN: 978–1–782–95873–4

All correspondence to:
Red Fox, Penguin Random House Children's
One Embassy Gardens, 8 Viaduct Gardens
London SW11 7BW

FATHER CHRISTMAS
NEEDS A WEE!

Nicholas Allan

Red Fox

Father Christmas needs a wee,
He's been drinking drinks since half past three!

At number 1 . . .

ONE hot choc, yum!

TWO plates of stew.

At number 3
THREE cups of tea,

At number 4
he'd had FOUR more!

At number 5
FIVE pops
(with pies!),

At number 6

fruit mix (all SIX).

At number 7 milk,

SEVEN, pure heaven!

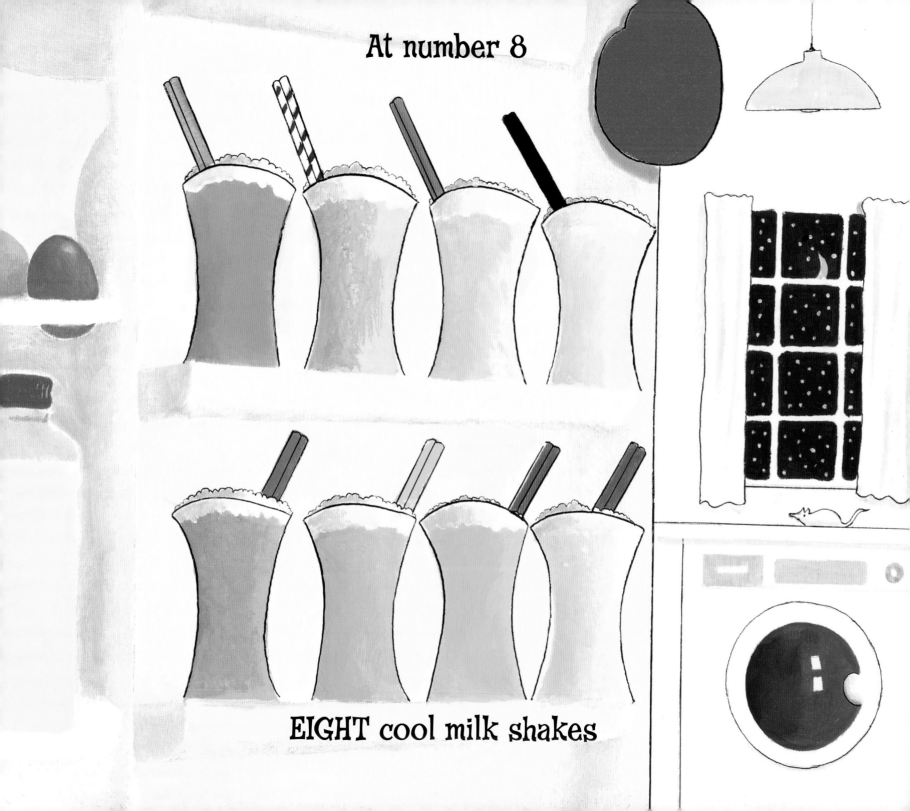

At number 8

EIGHT cool milk shakes

NINE lemon and limes.

TEN teas . . . and THEN . . .

But, oh! What with all those drinks in mind . . .

he forgot to leave the presents behind! And SO . . .

At number 10 he left TEN pens,

At number 9 NINE nursery rhymes.

At number 8 EIGHT pairs of skates,

At number 7 sweets! SEVEN, *more* heaven!

At number 6 SIX colourful bricks,

At number 5 FIVE toys to drive.

At number 4 FOUR beasts that ROAR!

At number 3 THREE Christmas trees.

At number 2 TWO cows that . . .

MOOOOOO!

At number 1 ONE pup that RUNS!

And so, at last, his work is done!

And now it's time for him to flee,

For Father Christmas needs a wee!

Through the town, across the sky,
The sledge it rises, rises high!

Above the clouds and over the sea.
He must be quick, he needs his wee!

At last he's back, at home, all safe,

Just *look* at that smile upon his face!

He feels in his pocket – but *where* is the key?
For Father Christmas NEEDS A WEE!

An elf with a gift appears by the door,

"I found this key - just here, on the floor."

He thanks the elf, and turns the lock,

He runs up the stairs, right up to the top.

And there is the loo, he shuts the door . . .

"Oh, Happy Christmas!"

we hear him roar!